Karen Adrian has been a preschool teacher for almost 20 years. She has a book published by Amazon titled *Tomorrow Will Come,* using her maiden name, Curran. She is a mother of five and a grandma of ten. She lives in Laporte with her husband Garry, dog Mojo, and cat Callie.

# CALEB, THE ICE ROAD TRUCK

## KAREN ADRIAN

**Austin Macauley Publishers™**
LONDON • CAMBRIDGE • NEW YORK • SHARJAH

# Copyright © Karen Adrian (2019)

All rights reserved. No part of this publication may be reproduced, distributed, or transmitted in any form or by any means, including photocopying, recording, or other electronic or mechanical methods, without the prior written permission of the publisher, except in the case of brief quotations embodied in critical reviews and certain other noncommercial uses permitted by copyright law. For permission requests, write to the publisher.

Any person who commits any unauthorized act in relation to this publication may be liable to criminal prosecution and civil claims for damages.

**Ordering Information:**
Quantity sales: special discounts are available on quantity purchases by corporations, associations, and others. For details, contact the publisher at the address below.

**Publisher's Cataloging-in-Publication data**
Adrian, Karen
Caleb, the Ice Road Truck

ISBN 9781645751274 (Paperback)
ISBN 9781645751267 (Hardback)
ISBN 9781645751281 (ePub e-Book)

Library of Congress Control Number: 2019918027

The main category of the book — JUVENILE FICTION / Action & Adventure / General

www.austinmacauley.com/us

First Published (2019)
Austin Macauley Publishers LLC
40 Wall Street, 28th Floor
New York, NY 10005
USA

mail-usa@austinmacauley.com
+1 (646) 5125767

I dedicate this book to Caleb, my dog. He left us many years ago but will never be forgotten. He was a tough, protective, and sweet dog.

"Oh, no!" Caleb shouted. "I'm going too fast!"
Caleb tried to pump his brakes to slow down. He sighed, but he could feel himself slowing down.
Caleb had driven down this dangerous hill many times. But tonight the snow was so thick he couldn't see his headlights.
He had always been an ice road truck, since many years. He had driven on the worse ice roads in America and Canada.
But tonight he had to deliver his cargo of cables for oil drills. They had to be on sight by morning, no later. So the company sent Caleb because they knew he would get the job done.

The wind was blowing snow so hard and fast that Caleb couldn't see anything at all. It was a total white out. His load would move back and forth with the wind, making it very dangerous on icy roads. Caleb fought to keep his tires on the road and not go over the 200 foot drop. He kept a close eye on the side of the road, even though he couldn't see it too well. Orange flags were placed about every 2–3 feet on the side of the road. So he made sure he didn't get too close to the flags. "Whoa…" Caleb let out a soft whistle, "I'm too close to the side of the road."

He tried to peek over the edge of the mountain, but all he could see was white. "Come in, Caleb," Jody, the dispatcher, called on the radio.
"I'm here. What's up?"
"The weather is getting worse in your area. You're headed right for the worst part of the storm."
"Great! I can't see anything now. How much worse can it get?"
"Weather service is shutting down the ice road. You're the only one who is still traveling."
"I can't stop now. Temperature is -20, I'll freeze overnight. I have to keep going." Caleb saw no other way but to keep moving forward.

"How far are you from us?"
"About 20 miles."
"You don't have any choice. Just be careful. I'll check in with you every half hour or so."
"Sounds great!" Caleb said.
He hung up his radio, said a silent prayer, and kept moving.
He knew he was coming up on the Roller Coaster Road. It was two miles of ups and downs. One drop was a good 30 feet straight down. He wanted to shift into a lower gear, but knew shifting on this steep hill would send him over the hill. So he had to keep his pace constant all the way down.

"Whoa! What a ride!" Caleb shouted. As he picked up speed, he kept his brake on so he wouldn't go too fast. He could feel his back tires wanting to slide back and forth, but with his brake on he was able to control the tires. He was finally able to make it safely to the bottom of the first and worst of the hills.

"Yes, at the bottom of the hill!" Caleb sighed. But he didn't have long to rest, the next hill was coming up fast. He climbed up and rode down the next two hills exactly as he did the first one.

"Jody, are you there?"
"I'm here. Glad to hear from you. Are you okay?"
"Yeah, did a little slipping and sliding, but I made it. Should be back in town within an hour or two. Is the storm letting up?"
"No, it is still going strong. Keep in touch; slow and easy is the way to go."
"See you soon."
"We'll have a warm garage 7 ready for you," Jody said.
Caleb drove slowly, the speed limit was only 25 miles an hour for this part of town.

It was nice to see streetlights and feel pavement again.
After he dropped off his cargo, he drove to garage 7 and sighed as he entered the warmth and comfort.

"Jody, it is nice to be out of the weather. I am safe and sound in number 7. Thanks for all the help tonight."

"Glad you are safe and sound. Sleep well tonight."
But Caleb didn't hear her, he had fallen fast asleep.

CPSIA information can be obtained
at www.ICGtesting.com
Printed in the USA
LVHW070652181021
700725LV00012B/1032